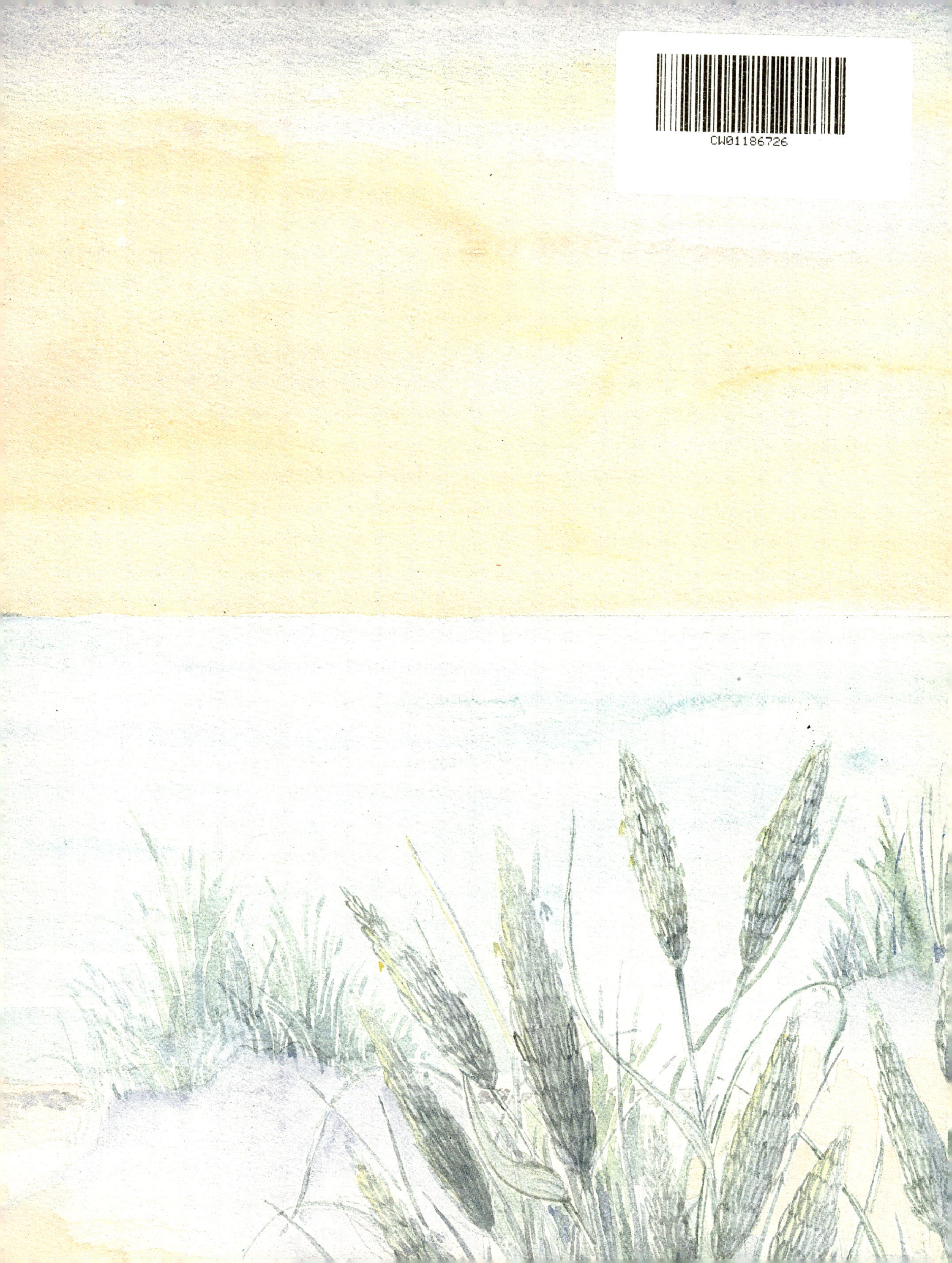

Also by Jan Mogensen
Just Before Dawn
Ted and the Chinese Princess
Mary's Christmas Present
Lost and Found

First published in Great Britain 1985
Published by Hamish Hamilton Children's Books
Garden House   57–59 Long Acre   London WC2E 9JZ
Copyright © Jan Mogensen 1984
English text copyright © Hamish Hamilton Ltd 1985
Published by arrangement with Borgen, Copenhagen
All Rights Reserved

British Library Cataloguing in Publication Data
Mogensen, Jan
Ted's seaside adventure
I. Title
II. Eventyr på havets bund *English*
839.8'1374 [J]   PZ7

ISBN 0-241-11560-4

Typeset by Katerprint Co. Ltd, Oxford
Printed in Denmark

Jan Mogensen

Ted's Seaside Adventure

Hamish Hamilton · London

One day, Ted went to the seaside with Jack and Mary. While they splashed about in the water, Ted stayed on the beach. He was a little afraid of the water.

"You never know what might be under the sea," he thought. "There might be a crab waiting to pinch your toe!"

Ted felt hot and sleepy in the sun. Slowly his eyes closed and he drifted off to sleep.

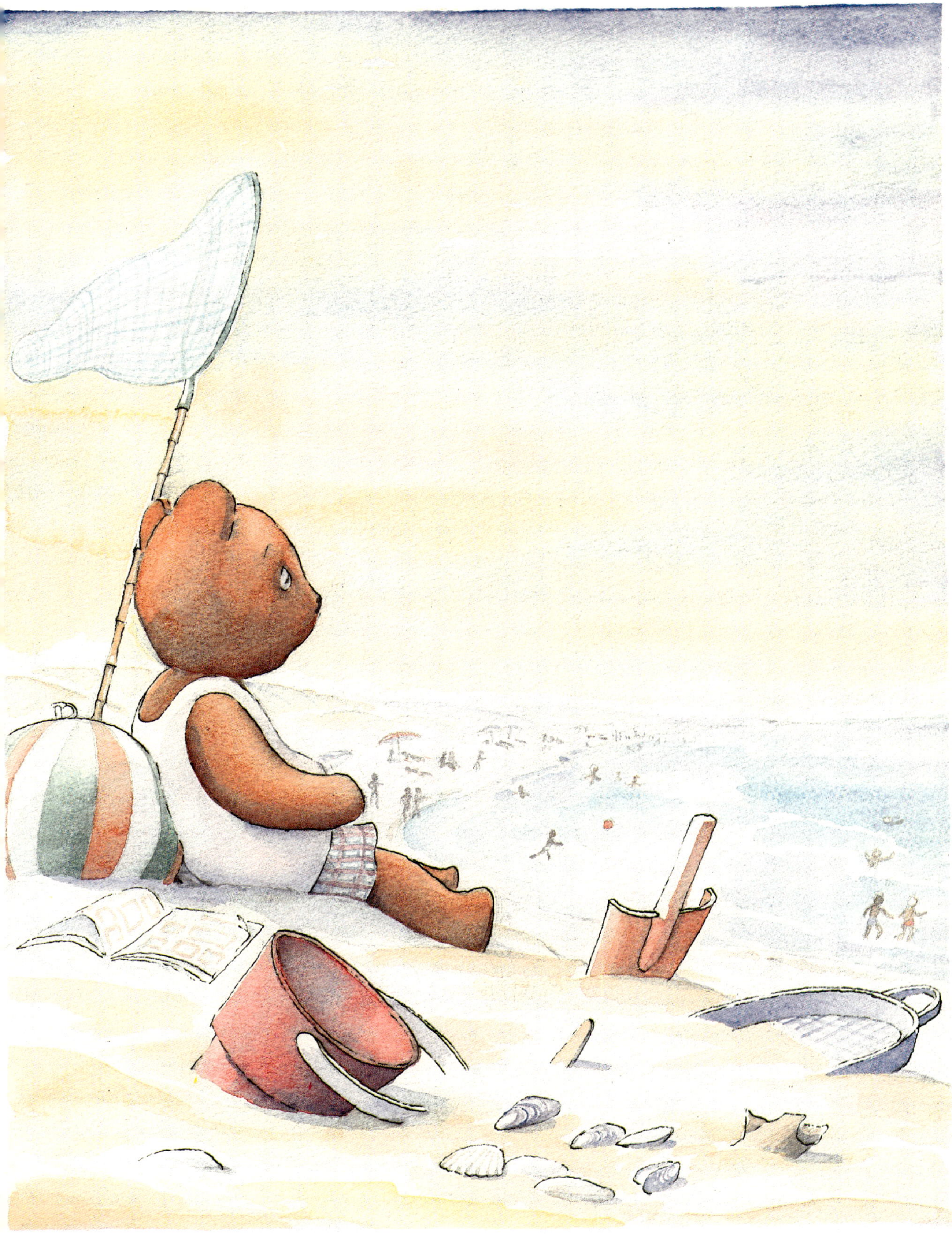

Suddenly Ted felt he was all alone. The sun was setting and the air was very still all around him.

"Where are Jack and Mary?" Ted wondered.

He picked up his bucket and fishing net and walked towards the water.

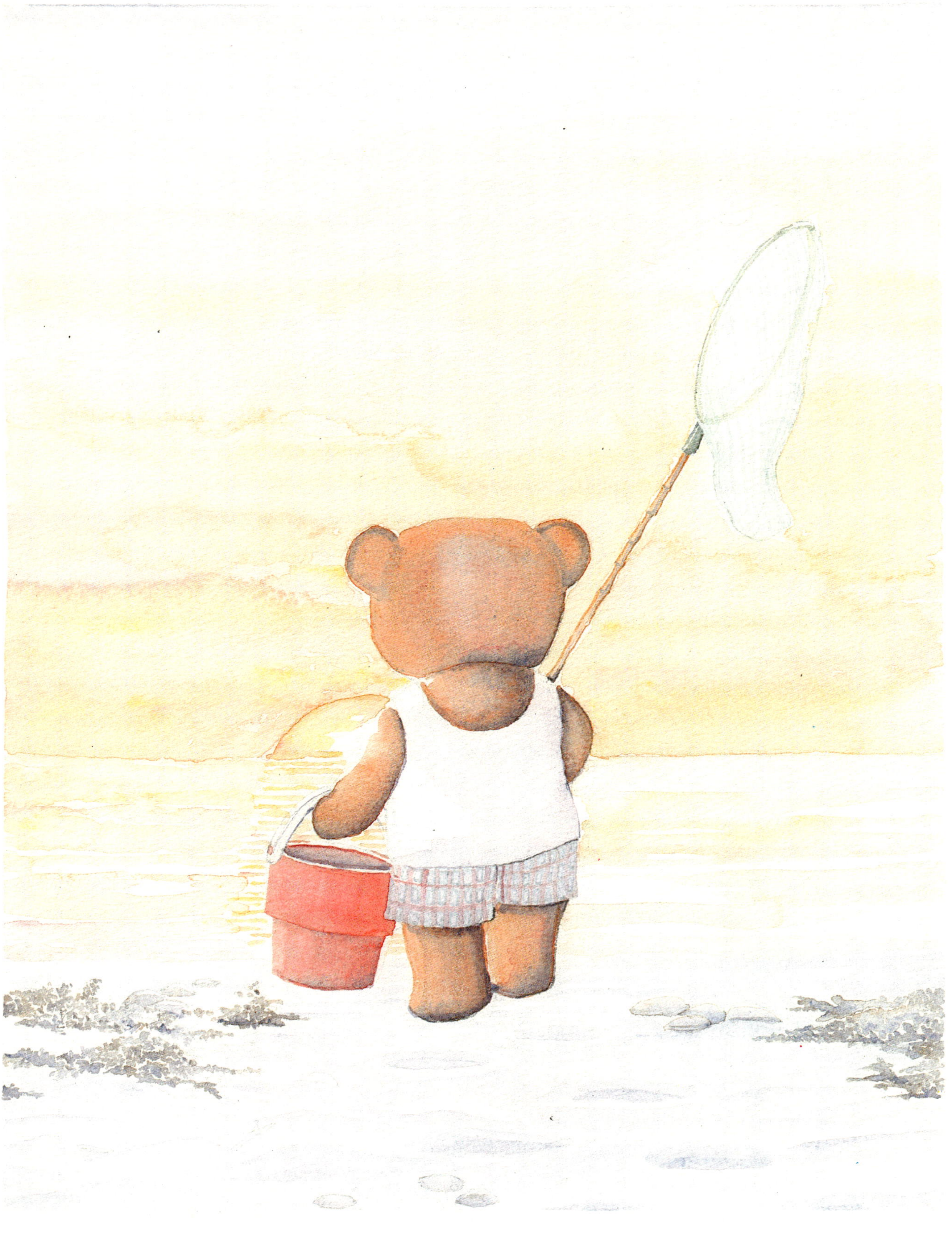

Ted stopped to pick up a shell. Then he saw a stone shining in the sand.

"Maybe it is made of gold," Ted thought as he picked it up.

Then Ted saw something sparkling like a diamond. All around he saw shells and pieces of glass and stones that glittered and shone. He was so excited he did not notice he was going farther and farther along the beach.

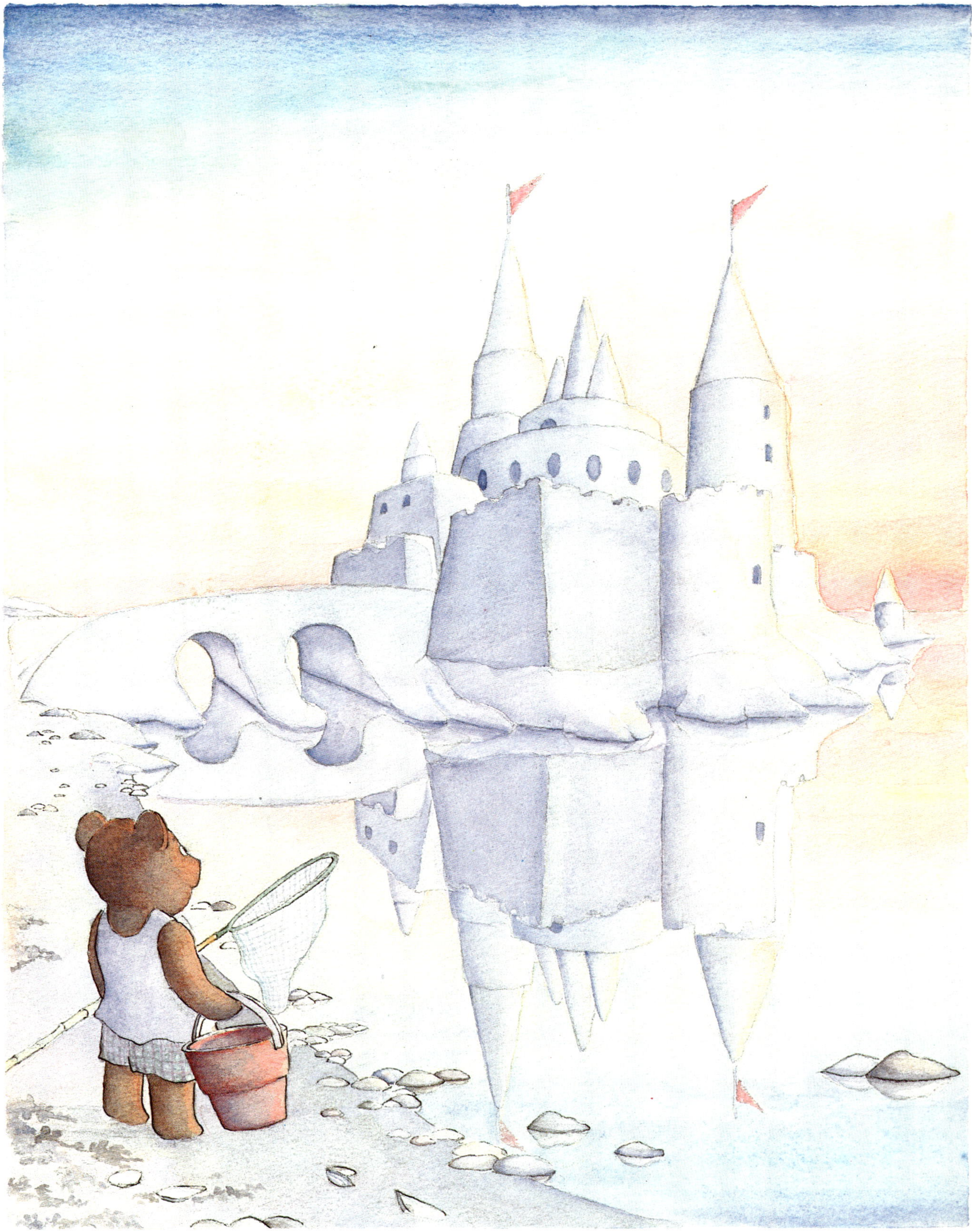

Then, when he stood up straight, he saw a huge sand castle with tall towers and pointed roofs. It seemed to float on the water. A splendid bridge stretched from the castle to the beach.

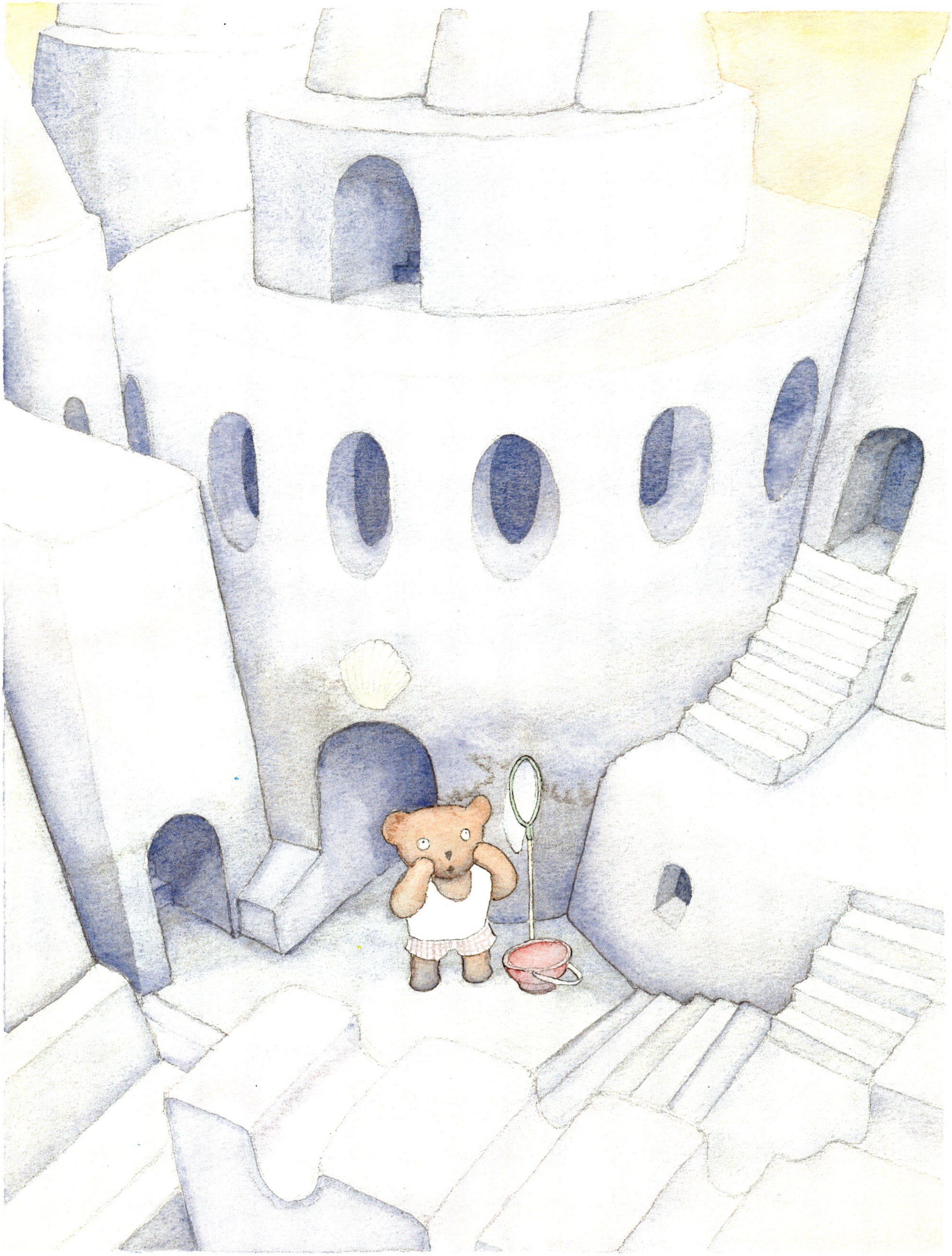

Ted went into the castle and looked around in wonder.

"Hello! Is anybody there?" he shouted.

Then he thought that far away he could hear the sound of somebody crying.

Ted found himself in a large hall. At the top of a flight of steps the shell King and shell Queen sat on shell thrones. It was the King and Queen who were crying.

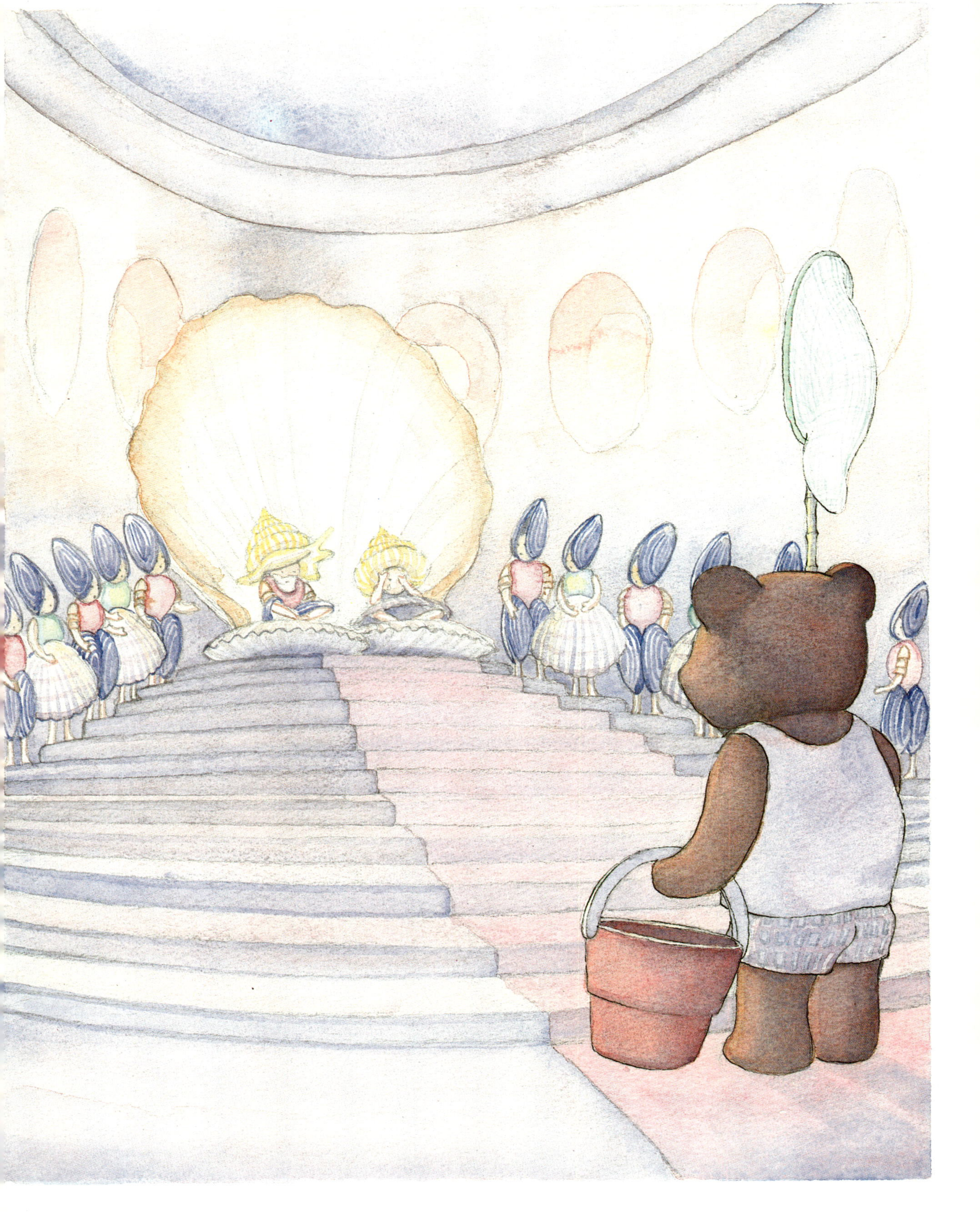

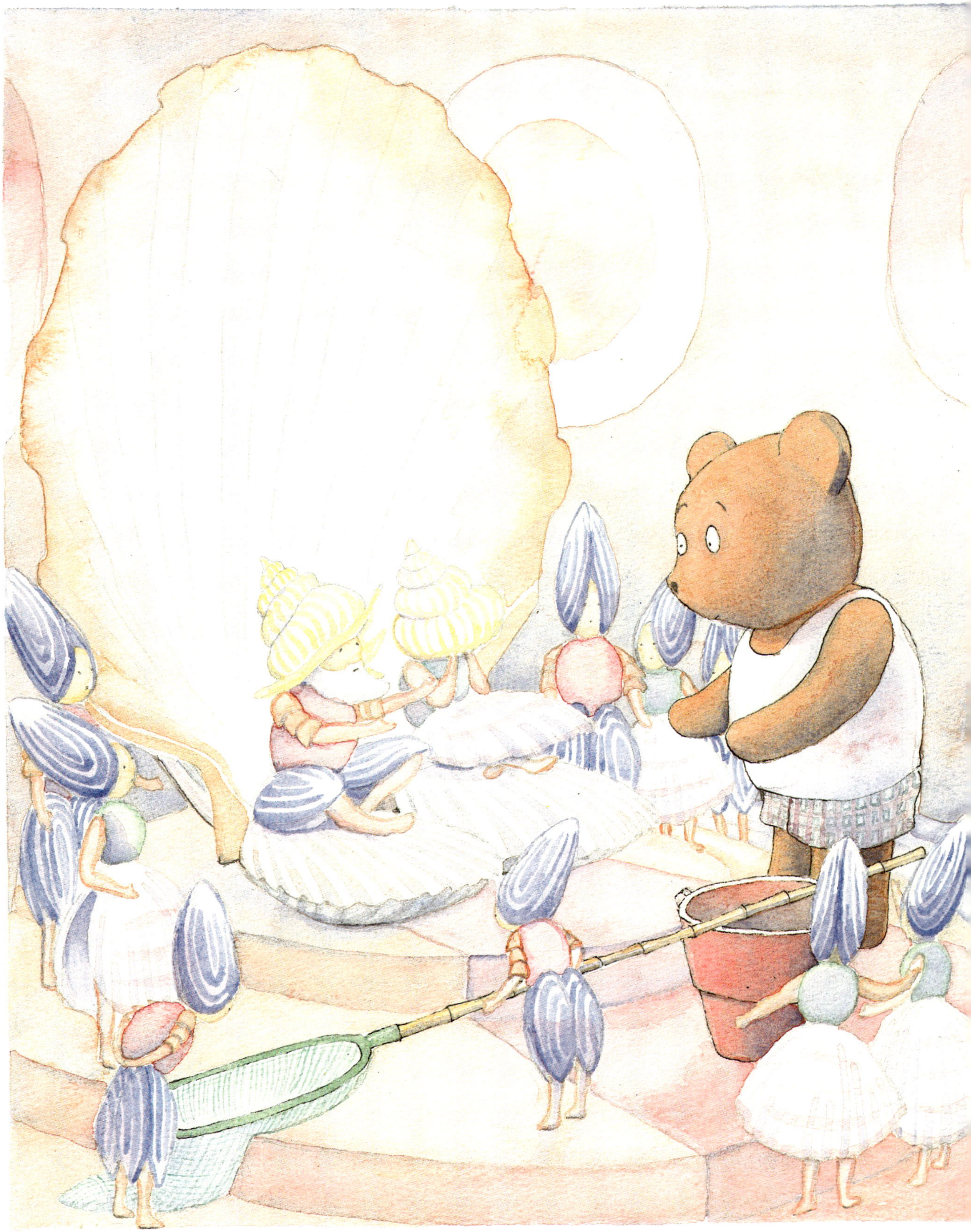

Ted said hello politely. Then he asked, "Why are you unhappy?"

The King looked at Ted sadly. "The wicked crab has stolen our youngest daughter. She is a prisoner in his cave at the bottom of the sea."

"The wicked crab will not get away with it," Ted said bravely. "Give me a fish to carry me and I shall rescue your daughter."

The King and the Queen and all the shell people cheered and waved as Ted set off on his adventure.

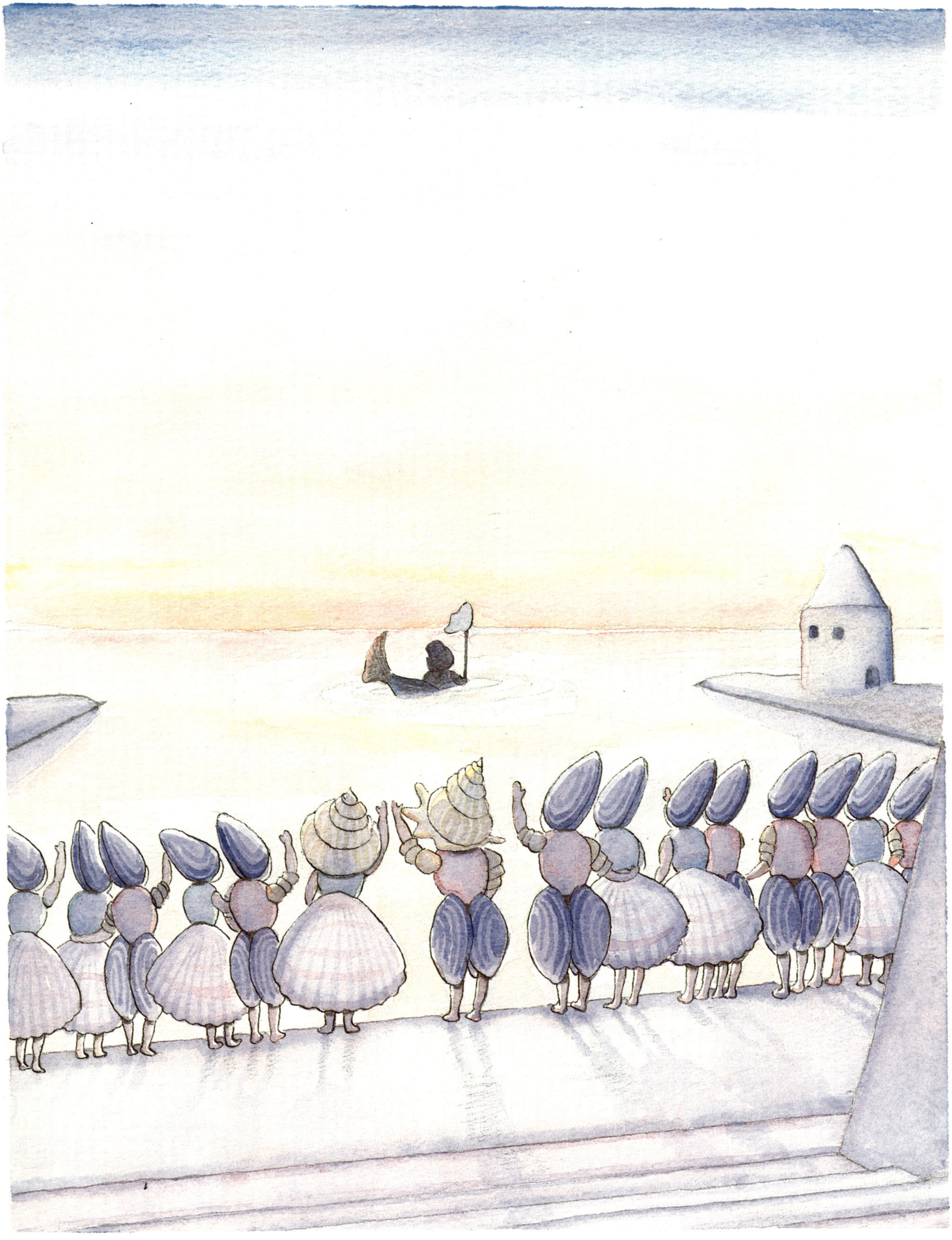

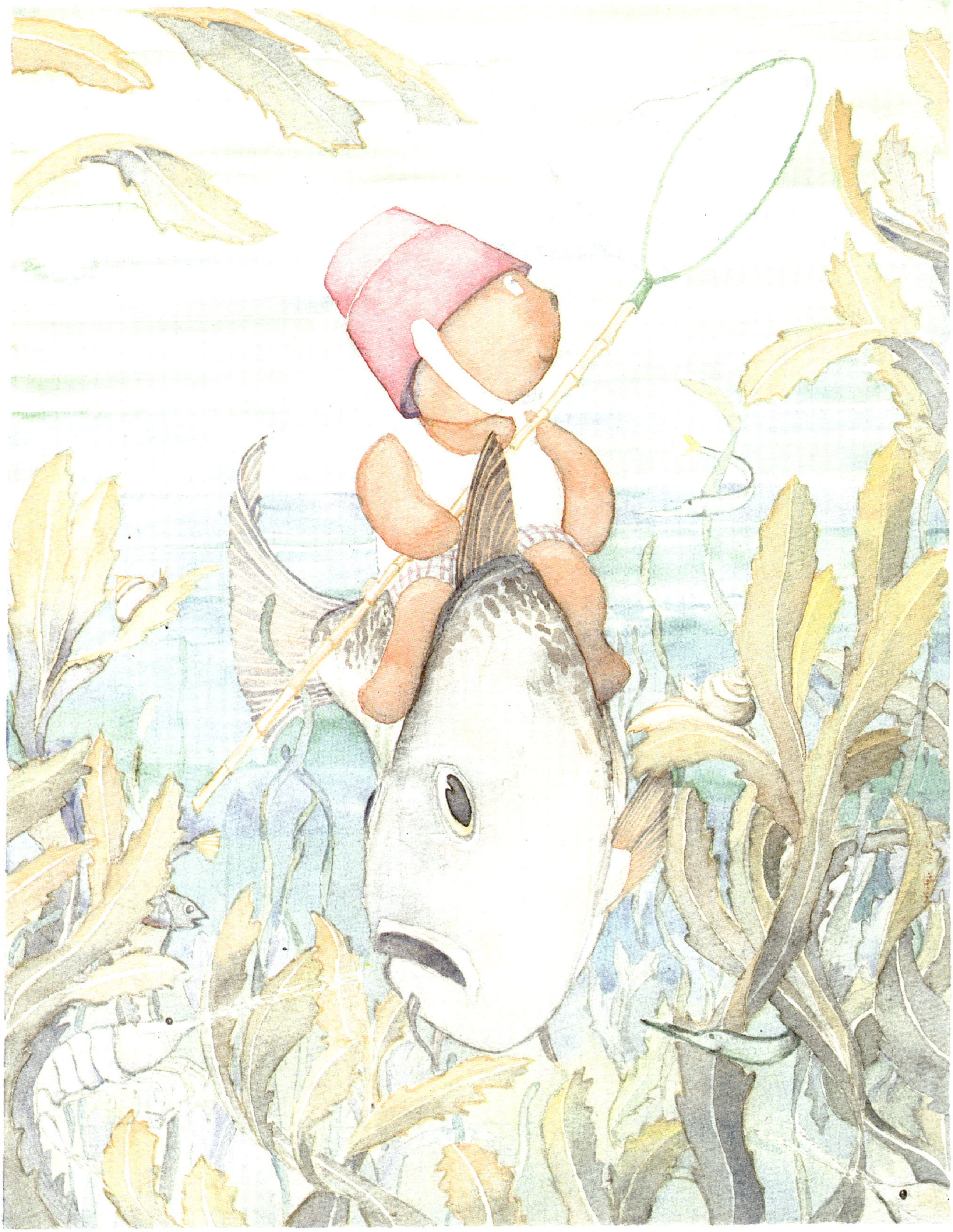

After Ted and the fish had been swimming for a while, they found themselves among some strange plants.

"That is the seaweed forest," the fish said. "The wicked crab's cave is in the middle of the forest."

At last they reached the crab's cave. "You will have to go the rest of the way alone," the fish whispered.

At the entrance to the cave, Ted laid his fishing net on the sea bed and covered it with sand. Then he shouted at the top of his voice,

"Let the princess go, you wicked crab!"

The crab rushed from his cave to find out who had shouted at him.

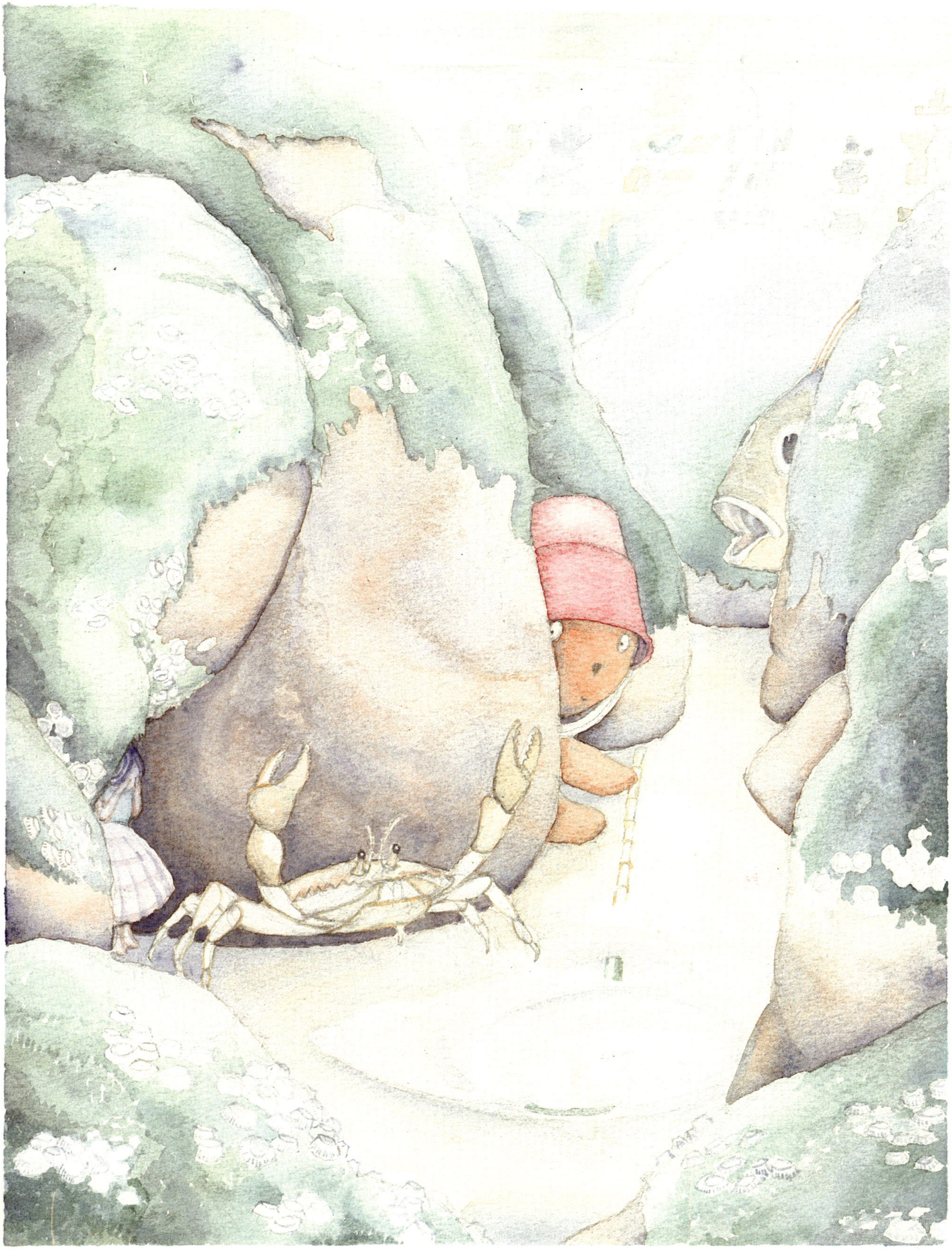

Just as the crab walked over the net, Ted raised it quickly and caught the crab. Ted picked up the shell princess and clambered onto the fish's back.

Before the crab could stop them, they swam away to safety.

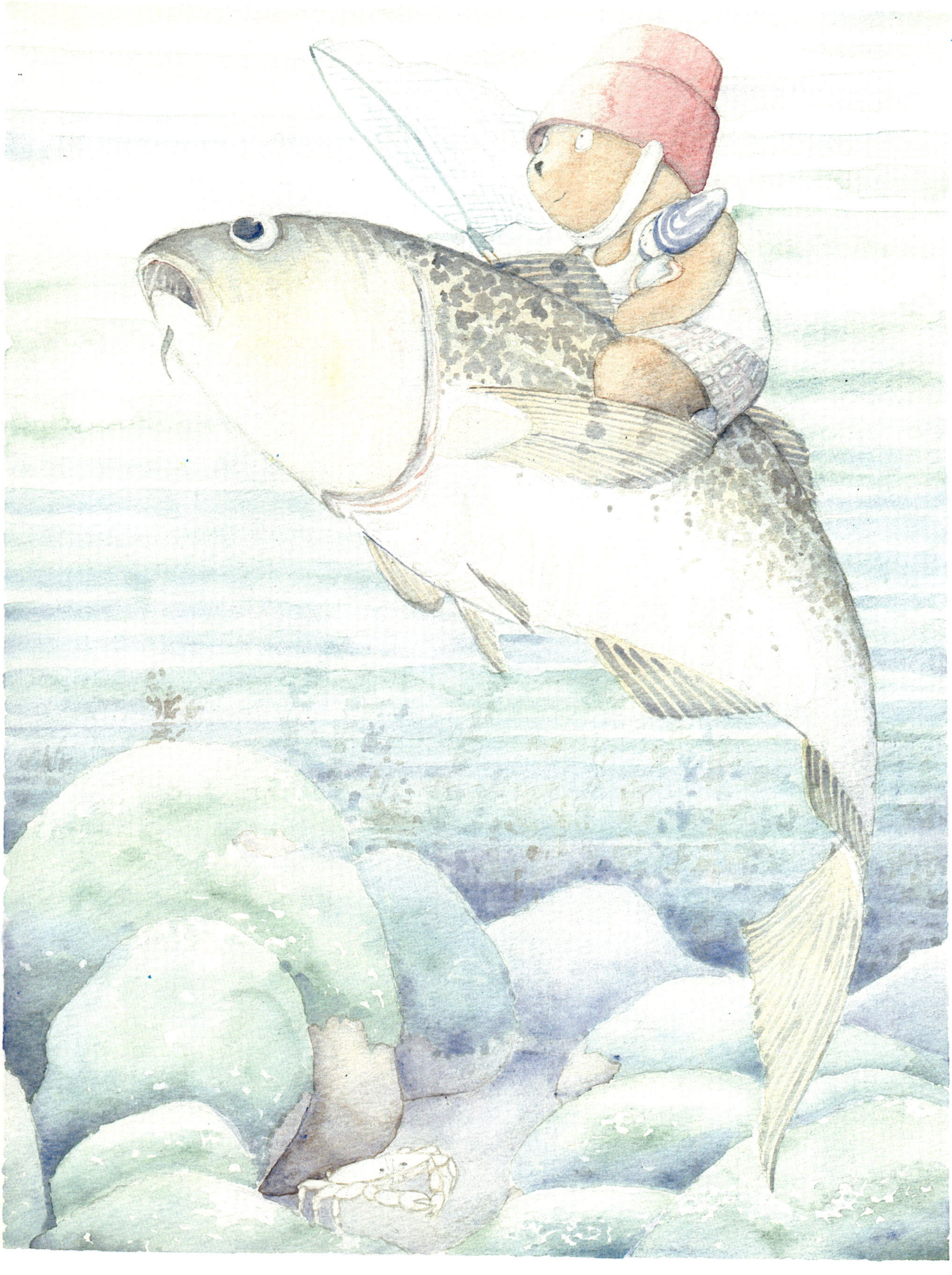

When they got back to the castle, all the shell people were waiting.

The Queen hugged her daughter. The King took off his crown and gave it to Ted.

The shell people threw their hats in the air and cheered.

"Three cheers for Ted!" they shouted.

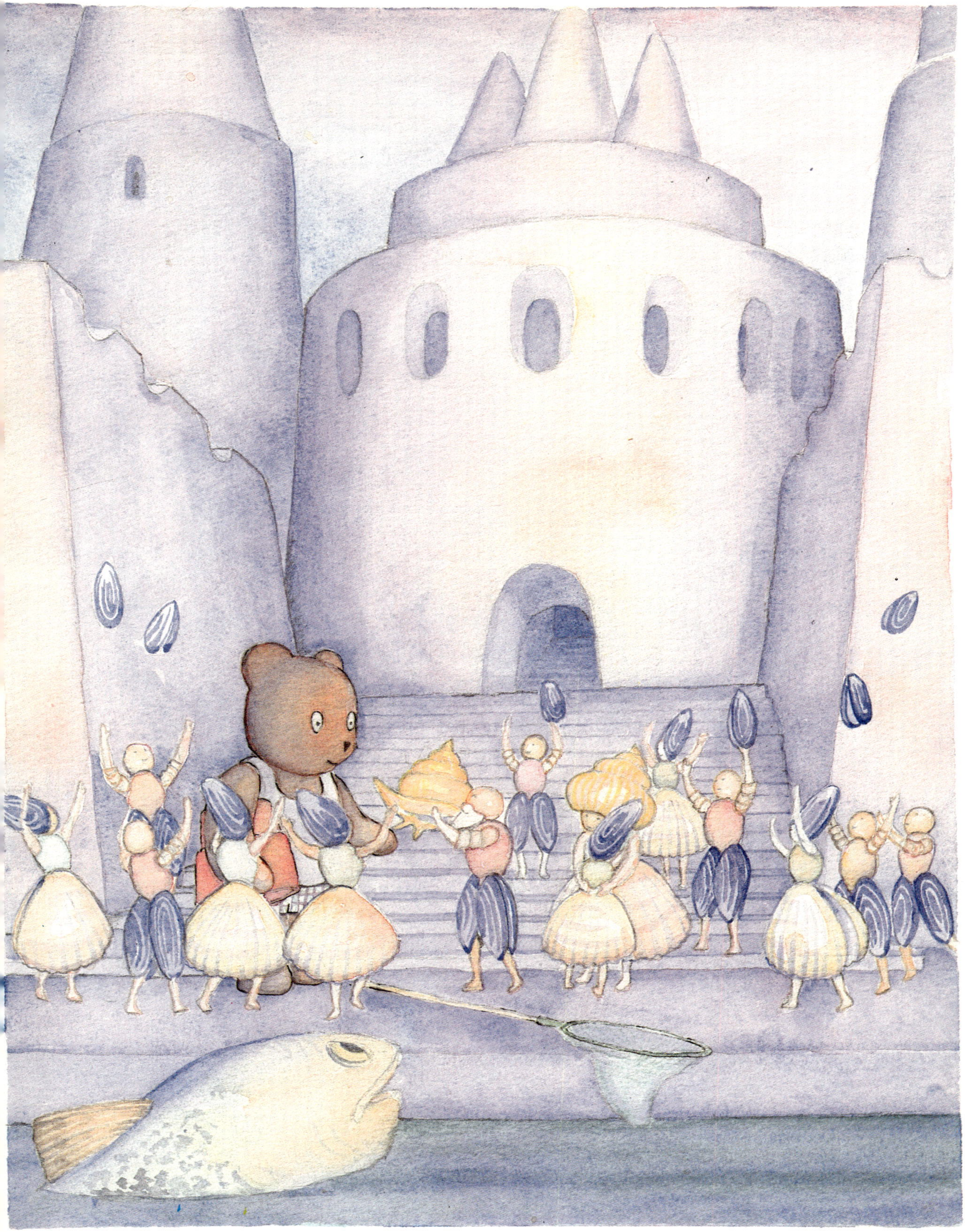

Then Ted heard a voice he knew. He opened his eyes and there was Mary with a large shell in her hands.

"Look what we have found Ted," Mary said. "Hold it to your ear and you can hear it whisper."

"Yes," Ted thought. "It whispers stories from the bottom of the sea."